W9-CUE-014

Galileo and the "Starry Messenger"

H. B. Hall and Stephanie Paris

Publishing Credits

Conni Medina, M.A.Ed., *Managing Editor*
Lee Aucoin, *Creative Director*
Diana Kenney, M.A.Ed., NBCT, *Senior Editor*
Christine Kinkopf, *Assistant Editor*
Hillary Dunlap, *Designer*
Rachelle Cracchiolo, M.S.Ed., *Publisher*

Image Credits: Cover, p.1 Bridgeman Art
Library; pp. 3, 7–24 Wikipedia; all other images
Shutterstock.

Teacher Created Materials
5301 Oceanus Drive
Huntington Beach, CA 92649-1030
http://www.tcmpub.com
ISBN 978-1-4807-4453-0
© 2015 Teacher Created Materials, Inc.

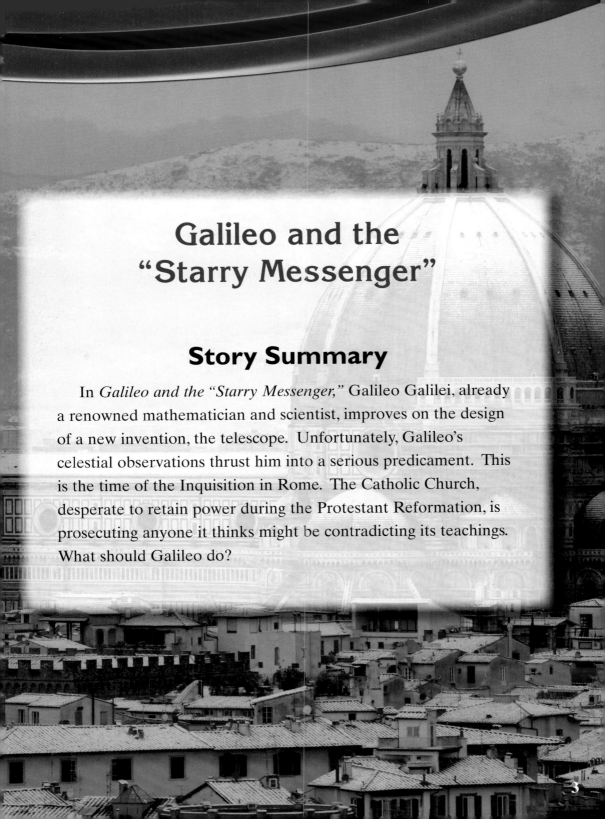

Galileo and the "Starry Messenger"

Story Summary

In *Galileo and the "Starry Messenger,"* Galileo Galilei, already a renowned mathematician and scientist, improves on the design of a new invention, the telescope. Unfortunately, Galileo's celestial observations thrust him into a serious predicament. This is the time of the Inquisition in Rome. The Catholic Church, desperate to retain power during the Protestant Reformation, is prosecuting anyone it thinks might be contradicting its teachings. What should Galileo do?

Tips for Performing Reader's Theater

Adapted from Aaron Shepard

★ Don't let your script hide your face. If you can't see the audience, your script is too high.

★ Look up often when you speak. Don't just look at your script.

★ Talk slowly so the audience knows what you are saying.

★ Talk loudly so everyone can hear you.

★ Talk with feelings. If the character is sad, let your voice be sad. If the character is surprised, let your voice be surprised.

★ Stand up straight. Keep your hands and feet still.

Tips for Performing Reader's Theater *(cont.)*

★ Remember that even when you are not talking, you are still your character.

★ If the audience laughs, wait for them to stop before you speak again.

★ If someone in the audience talks, don't pay attention.

★ If someone walks into the room, don't pay attention.

★ If you make a mistake, pretend it was right.

★ If you drop something, try to leave it where it is until the audience is looking somewhere else.

★ If a reader forgets to read his or her part, see if you can read the part instead, make something up, or just skip over it. Don't whisper to the reader!

Galileo and the "Starry Messenger"

Characters

Galileo Galilei

Father Paolo Sarpi

Sister Maria Celeste

Johannes Kepler

Grand Duchess
Christina de Medici

Roberto Bellarmino

Setting

This reader's theater is set in 1609 in Renaissance Italy. Galileo Galilei lives in a small but comfortable villa, furnished with scientific oddities and scattered with notes. Grand Duchess Christina de Medici's home is much more grand, filled with rich and luxurious furnishings and abundant art.

Act I

Father Paolo:	Professor Galileo, well met! And this is your daughter, Virginia, I presume? I understand you have taken your vows, my dear.
Sister Maria:	Father Paolo, I am now known as Sister Maria Celeste. I took the new name to honor my father's love of astronomy.
Father Paolo:	Wonderful! In fact, Professor Galileo, it is your love of astronomy that has brought me here today. Have you heard of this new invention, the telescope?
Galileo:	As I understand it, the device is a sort of cylinder set with a series of parallel lenses. Each lens magnifies the light of the one before it. A person looking through one end can see distant objects at several times the size at which they appear on the horizon. A man might look at a ship out at sea and spot the flag it flies. Or, one might turn the lenses toward the heavens and learn more about the universe. Is it not so?
Father Paolo:	You are quite right, as always, my friend!
Galileo:	I would dearly love to inspect its intricacies.
Father Paolo:	I believe that can be arranged.
Sister Maria:	Oh, Father Paolo, are you implying that the telescope is still in the area? The two of you could travel to study it!
Father Paolo:	I have arranged for something even better, I think.

Galileo: Better, my friend? What could be better than closely inspecting such an amazing object?

Father Paolo: I was thinking perhaps you would like to construct a telescope of your own.

Sister Maria: Build a telescope? Oh Illustrious Father, do you believe you could really build such an instrument?

Galileo: Hmmm. Yes, I imagine I could. I would need to experiment, though. And that requires investments. The Medici family has supported me with similar endeavors…

Father Paolo: That is what I have come to tell you. The owner of the telescope came to Venice to sell the invention, but I spoke to the Venetian government on your behalf. I convinced them that you can create a telescope as good as the one being offered.

Sister Maria: Oh, how incredibly kind of you to speak on my father's behalf!

Galileo: Father Paolo, do not tell me that you have secured contracts from the city of Venice! I am not even certain that I can make this invention work.

Father Paolo: All right, I will not tell you.

Galileo: Thank heavens. That is a relief.

Sister Maria: Dearest Father, I believe that Father Paolo is having a jest with us. He means that he has, in fact, gotten the contracts. Is that not correct, Father Paolo?

Father Paolo: Of course I have, because I have every confidence in you, Professor Galileo! And, I might add, so do the city leaders of Venice. Your work with pendulums has gained you quite a lot of fame, my friend!

Galileo: I shall do my best to match my distinguished reputation.

Sister Maria: When will you commence?

Galileo: At once! Father Paolo, Daughter, please excuse me. I suddenly have much work to do.

Act 2

Sister Maria: Most Illustrious Lord Father, you must rest. It has been numerous months since you created the new telescope. From what I gather, it is considered to be better than any that was created before. You should enjoy your success!

Galileo: But, I am enjoying it! I take great pleasure in using my own invention to learn more about the universe. Why, I have even discovered not one, but four moons circling Jupiter. Do you know what this discovery means?

Sister Maria: I have been meaning to talk with you regarding that. I have some concerns that the Church will not graciously receive that particular aspect of your work.

Galileo: Yes, I understand what you are implying. If there are moons around Jupiter, then everything does not circle Earth. Copernicus may have been right with his theories!

Sister Maria: Hush, Father, please do not discuss these matters so openly. It is a very serious thing to go against the Church. The last thing I should ever wish is for you to be brought before the Inquisition.

Galileo: Do not fear, Daughter. I am not naive. I have taken certain precautions with the most controversial aspects of my inquiries.

☙☙

Kepler: Professor Galileo, well met! We have much to discuss, my honored colleague.

Galileo: Professor Kepler, I am very glad to see you. But, I did not expect this impromptu visit all the way from Germany. Were you unable to decipher my most recent letter?

Kepler: I had no trouble reading your writing. However, I am afraid our coded letters do not allow a truly deep discussion of your recent findings.

Sister Maria: Father, you had expressed to me that you were communicating with this renowned astronomer, but I did not realize you were writing in code! Please explain to me how it works.

Kepler: Oh, we have quite a fun little code in which we switch letters around. For instance, your father once wrote to me about his discovery that Saturn has two smaller companions that move with it. He wrote *Smaismrmilmepoetaleumibunenugttaviras*.

Sister Maria: Oh my goodness, that sounds incredibly complex!

Kepler: Nonsense, Sister, can you not see? It is easily unscrambled into *Altissimum planetam tergeminum observavi,*—"I have observed the highest of the planets three-formed." We scientists love to play with anagrams. It helps keep our discoveries secret until we are ready to publish them fully.

Sister Maria:	How very clever of you both!
Kepler:	Ah, you will have to search far and wide to find two more clever men than we are, Sister!
Galileo:	Oh, do not listen to him, Daughter. We are merely ridiculous old men with our eyes toward the heavens.
Kepler:	Indeed, it is the heavens that I have come to discuss. I desire to know your thoughts on Copernicus's model of the universe. Has your viewing of Jupiter's satellites changed your mind? Will you go public with your views and publish that it is the sun, not Earth that is at the center of things?
Galileo:	Like you, I accepted the Copernican position years ago. From that, I have discovered dozens of natural effects, which were inexplicable before. I have written many articles on the subject. But, I have not dared to publish them. Consider Copernicus. The well-educated few honor him. But, among many, he is derided and dishonored. The foolish are numerous. If I had many thoughts, like you, I would publish them. But my ideas are few, so I will wait.
Kepler:	I truly wish that you would choose another course of action. You have such profound insight! The assertion that Earth moves can no longer be considered a new theory. Should we not join our powerful voices to shout down the herd? We should allow ourselves to be vulnerable in order to oppose the violent attacks from the mob of scholars. They do not weigh the arguments very carefully. Through cleverness we can bring knowledge of the truth.

Galileo:	Professor Kepler, you realize I am a devout Catholic. It is a fine line that I walk to be true to my science and true to my pope. I have gotten encouragement recently from the Vatican. However, I still fear the response of our peers.
Kepler:	Be of good cheer, Galileo! Speak out publicly. If I judge correctly, only a few of the distinguished mathematicians of Europe would part company with you. The power of truth is great. If Italy does not seem a good place for your publication, consider publishing in Germany instead.
Galileo:	I shall consider your advice. In the meantime, I shall publish a small pamphlet about my latest findings.
Kepler:	Such an astronomical editorial cannot be that trivial, my dear friend. From what I can ascertain, you have been making discoveries faster than you can possibly report them. But, do not keep us in suspense! Tell us quickly, what will you name your pamphlet?
Galileo:	I shall title it *Starry Messenger*.

Act 3

Poem: Every planet above, and every star

| Father Paolo: | Good evening, Your Serene Highness, that is such a romantic verse. Is it not from Gaspara Stampa? |

Grand Duchess: Indeed it is, Father Paolo. I memorized the poem during my younger years. *(to Galileo)* The planets and stars were much more mysterious before your telescopes, Professor Galileo. They had the characteristics of those old Gods, for which they were named. This touches on why I invited you here this evening. I wish to discuss a letter you sent me, Professor Galileo. In the letter, you defend your scientific findings against those who call them heretical.

Galileo: As Your Serene Highness knows, I have discovered many things. Many professors have been stirred up, as if I had placed these things in the sky in order to overturn the sciences.

Father Paolo: Instead of reviewing Galileo's work themselves, these professors made charges. They published many works filled with useless arguments. They then used passages from the Bible as proof—which I believe they had failed to properly grasp.

Galileo: Grand Duchess, these professors know I hold the sun to be still while Earth moves. My new findings plainly agree with and confirm a sun-centered universe.

Grand Duchess: Professor, these men were taught that everything revolves around Earth—the Ptolemaic (tol-uh-MEY-ik) system. It is what they have understood since childhood, and what the Church has acknowledged. Do you expect them to admit what they have been taught is actually erroneous?

Galileo: These men use false interpretations of the Bible to refute what they do not understand. They try to make this new opinion belong to me alone. They pretend not to know that its author was Nicholas Copernicus, and that he was not only a Catholic, but also a priest and a canon.

Grand Duchess: Yes, yes, some of your detractors do ignore the works of Copernicus. Very few people have had the time or opportunity to study the skies. They do not know about new instruments, like your telescope, that you use to better see the planets and stars.

Father Paolo: The reason they give for condemning the idea that Earth moves and the sun stands still, is that the Bible states the reverse. Since the Bible cannot err, it follows that anyone who thinks the contrary is taking a heretical position.

Grand Duchess: Do you believe this position to be incorrect?

Father Paolo: With regard to this debate, many think it is moral to say that the Holy Bible can never speak an untruth. But Galileo thinks, and nobody will deny, that the Bible is often very obscure. It may imply things that are quite different from what its words actually state.

Grand Duchess: Gentlemen, I understand that you share the opinion that, in discussions of physical problems, we ought to begin not from the authority of scriptural passages, but from experiences and demonstrations. But, this could be seen as in direct conflict with the need for Faith. I agree that the Bible, in order to be understood by every man, does say many things that appear to differ from the absolute truth. But are you to say that Nature is not changeable and never breaks the laws imposed upon her? This is in opposition to what many believe is God's Will. I fear this position may cause you trouble.

Father Paolo: Your position and counsel are both well considered and wise, Your Serene Highness. May Professor Galileo rest easier knowing he is assured your continued support?

Grand Duchess: Know that privately you will always have my support. Now I wish you both a safe journey home.

 Song: Twinkle, Twinkle, Little Star

Bellarmino: Greetings, Serene Highness Christina, Father Paolo, Sister Celeste, and Professor Kepler. I am glad that you are all willing to meet with me on such short notice. I have been charged by the pope to inquire about some controversial material in Professor Galileo's *Starry Messenger*.

Grand Duchess: Your Eminence, I am honored with your presence in my home. Any service we can render will be granted forthwith.

Bellarmino: I want to make it clear at the outset; the Church does not wish to harm the reputation of an esteemed man, such as Professor Galileo, without proper cause. However, there has been great concern regarding this latest publication of his. *Starry Messenger* has been highly recommended...

Grand Duchess: *(interrupting)* Oh, thank you, Cardinal Bellarmino. It is always pleasing when one's patronage is so well rewarded! Have you seen the amazing telescope that Professor Galileo has created?

Bellarmino: Er, no, Grand Duchess, I have not had that pleasure. However, in regards to *Starry Messenger*, surely the good professor did not mean to imply that Earth is not at the center of all things? That assertion would be completely against the teachings of the Church, as you know, and the Holy See would not be able to overlook such a breech.

Grand Duchess: Ah, yes. Well, I should say that even when one provides monetary support for an artist or scholar, one never does have much control over his work. I sincerely hope that a beneficiary of our charity has not brought dishonor.

Bellarmino: Of course, Grand Duchess. It is quite clear you are not responsible for Professor Galileo's writings. No one would, in any way, consider you to blame for his heretical views, if they are in fact heretical.

Sister Maria: Surely not heresy! I assure you, my father means no disrespect to the established views. His only interest is in truthfully reporting what he sees. He can only report what he can deduce based on his observations.

Bellarmino: I do not think that it is the reporting that has become a problem, but the interpretation that he brings to his findings.

Father Paolo: I am a scholar and a student of religion myself. I find Professor Galileo's observations quite informative. I have heard that a growing number of scholars are entertaining the idea that the heavens may be moving in a different dance than we had assumed. It is thrilling to live in a time when knowledge is growing so quickly!

Bellarmino: Be careful what you say, Father Paolo, the Church does not have room for deviance on this matter. While I myself have thought that this area needs further research, it is not the place of a scientist to speak against the Gospels!

Grand Duchess: I had a discussion with Professor Galileo about this very topic not long ago. There are, indeed, many of his colleagues who do not agree with his position.

Kepler: Those men are weak minded! Professor Galileo is hardly alone in his analyses on this matter. Many scholars have been convinced for years that the Copernican model of the universe is correct. In fact, I am convinced that it is a majority. But, some fear to come forward. I, for one, have urged my friend to speak publicly on his views. I believe his courageousness will set an example.

Bellarmino: Professor Kepler, your brazenness is not a help to your friend! It is this very thought that concerns the Vatican. In Germany, the land of Martin Luther, you may find your heretical views are condoned. But, this is Italy, and here we are more vigilant.

Sister Maria: Please, Cardinal, do not take Professor Kepler's views to be those of my father's. As you say, Germany and Italy are both lovely lands. However, Germany is a different place than Italy. Likewise, Professors Kepler and Galileo are both renowned men of science. However, they are not the same man!

Bellarmino: Your point is well taken, Sister. I will, of course, allow Professor Galileo to address the charges on his own behalf. I intended this meeting to be only advisory.

Kepler:	It is quite true, of course, that Professor Galileo and I do not always agree. For instance, I have been completely unable to convince him that the orbit of the planets is elliptical. The silly man is convinced that the orbit is circular! Can you imagine? Given all the evidence I have accrued, he still believes in a circular orbit of the planets!
Bellarmino:	I am sorry, Professor Kepler, can you repeat that? Did you just say that Professor Galileo believes that the planets are orbiting the sun? Has he gone over entirely to the Copernican model of the universe?
Grand Duchess:	Professor Kepler, I sincerely believe that you may be doing more harm than good with your strident support.
Kepler:	I beg all of your pardons. It is, of course, not my place to speak for the venerable Professor Galileo on a topic of such sensitivity to the Church.
Bellarmino:	Yes, again, the point is well taken. I am afraid that I do not come away from this meeting convinced of Professor Galileo's innocence; however, it is only equitable to speak with him in person before making my decision. Thank you all for coming.

Act 5

Bellarmino:	Professor Galileo, I have closely poured over your manuscript and spoken with your supporters and many of your detractors. But, I wish to hear your intentions firsthand. Will you speak out against the Ptolemaic view of the universe? Do you side with Copernicus on this matter?

Galileo:	To be honest, Your Eminence, I do not know what to do about my discoveries. Many parts of this information will help sailors in navigation. How can I stay silent?
Kepler:	My friend, I do not desire your situation. You know that I would have you publish all of your observations for the common good and the furtherance of scientific research. But, I have now seen firsthand the pressure exuded upon you.
Galileo:	Indeed, many professors and men in the Church are against me. I fear that this investigation will only be one of many.
Father Paolo:	You argue that those who oppose you are not well educated in astronomy and they err in their understanding of the Bible. But these arguments will not gain you any support. Some of these men hold great positions in high places.
Bellarmino:	Galileo, the Church supports an Earth-centered interpretation of the universe. The pope cannot and will not support the opposing Copernican model. It is a matter of faith, not science. My friend, step back from the issue and let the turmoil calm. Do not position yourself to be called a heretic.
Galileo:	Your Eminence, surely the Bible teaches how to go to heaven, not how the heavens go! The universe stands open to our gaze. It cannot be understood unless one first learns to comprehend the language. Its letters and words are mathematics. Without knowing this language, one is wandering about in a dark labyrinth.

Bellarmino: I caution you to choose your words, carefully, Professor Galileo. I shall leave you now to consider your position in private.

Father Paolo: My friend, you know that I have gone against Cardinal Bellarmino before. I believe the Church should have domain over all things spiritual. But, I believe nonspiritual things should be left to earthly authorities.

Kepler: Father Paolo, I had no idea that you were a reformer in disguise!

Father Paolo: I play the roles that I believe are necessary, Professor Kepler. But, Galileo my friend, I fear you have nothing to gain by battling the Cardinal on this matter. The Church, believe it or not, is in a similar position to yours. They feel increasing pressures from the new discoveries of the science community. You and I may be willing to quickly merge the new knowledge with our faith. But, the Church fears that others may not be so willing. What if they accept these new findings? With the scientific evidence against them, they fear they will lose power.

Sister Maria: My Illustrious Lord Father, perhaps there is a solution in selective silence. From what I have heard, the Church has been trying to avoid this conflict. But there are those who are eager to display the power of the pope to win his favor. I know you have been counseled by others to press forward, but I recommend that you continue your research quietly. Keep your discoveries close and private. Publish only those that could be beyond reproach.

Galileo: Sadly, you are correct, Daughter. I will still continue my research and exploration, but I will publish only my findings that will assist navigation. The rest will be shared only amongst friends. I fear it may already be too late for me, but I still have friends in high places that can help.

ൟ

Bellarmino: Professor Galileo, have you had time to reach a decision?

Father Paolo: My friend, Galileo, offers that he resume his research in a way that pleases the Church. He shall publish only details that will be helpful to navigation. He will not include anything that disproves Ptolemy, until such a time that the Church gives him permission to do so. Would this compromise be to your liking, Cardinal Bellarmino?

Bellarmino: I believe this proposition would be agreeable to all concerned. If this is truly your intent, Professor Galileo, I will go now to bring word to the Vatican.

Galileo: Yes, Your Eminence, I agree. Heavens help me, I agree.

Every planet above, and every star

by Gaspara Stampa

Every planet above, and every star,
Gave my lord their powers at his birth:
Each one gave him of their special worth,
To make a single perfect mortal here.
Saturn gave him depths of understanding,
Jupiter for fine actions gave desire,
Mars a greater skill than most in warfare,
Phoebus, elegance and wit in speaking.

Venus beauty too, and gentleness,
Mercury eloquence, but then the moon
Made him too cold for me, in iciness.
Each of these graces, each rare boon,
Make me burn for his fierce brightness,
And yet he freezes, through that one alone.

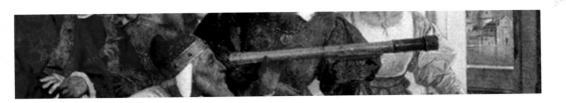

Twinkle, Twinkle, Little Star

by Ann and Jane Taylor

Twinkle, twinkle, little star,
How I wonder what you are!
Up above the world so high,
Like a diamond in the sky!

When the blazing sun is gone,
When he nothing shines upon,
Then you show your little light,
Twinkle, twinkle, all the night.

Then the traveller in the dark,
Thanks you for your tiny spark,
He could not see which way to go,
If you did not twinkle so.

In the dark blue sky you keep,
And often through my curtains peep,
For you never shut your eye,
'Till the sun is in the sky.

'Tis your bright and tiny spark,
Lights the traveller in the dark;—
Tho' I know not what you are,
Twinkle, twinkle, little star.

Glossary

anagrams—words or phrases made by changing the order of letters in another word or phrase

canon—a member of the clergy who is on the staff of a cathedral

derided—talked or written about in a very critical or insulting way

detractors—people who criticize something or someone

endeavors—serious efforts or attempts

erroneous—not correct

heresy—a belief or opinion that does not agree with the official belief or opinion of a particular religion

heretical—someone or something who believes or teaches something that goes against accepted or official beliefs

Holy See—"government" in Rome of the Catholic Church

illustrious—admired and respected for achievements

inexplicable—not able to be explained or understood

Inquisition—in the past, an organization in the Roman Catholic Church that was responsible for finding and punishing people who did not accept its beliefs and practices

pendulums—sticks with weights at the bottom that swing back and forth

venerable—valued and respected because of old age

well met—a greeting